QUIXOTE COYOTE
BY
JOSEPH MORRIS

WWW.TORCPRESS.COM

♪ ♪ ♪
WHAT'S THIS NOW?

AWW...WE'RE JUST HAVIN' FUN.
HEY! I KNOW YOU!
SQUEEL!

YOU'RE THAT QUIXOTE COYOTE, RIGHT? YER NAMED AFTER THAT GUY THAT ATTACKED WINDMILLS CAUSE HE THOUGHT THEY WUZ GIANTS. THAT WHAT YOU DO, SHRIMP? FIGHT GIANTS?
I DUNNO ABOUT GIANTS...
WHIMPER!

...BUT I KNOW A BULLY WHEN I SEE ONE!
POW

GIT BACK HERE YOU RUNT!
WELL, QUIXOTE COYOTE, THAT'S WHAT YOU GET FOR STANDING UP TO A BULLY...CHASED BY HIM & ALL HIS FRIENDS!

EAT TRASH, WOLF-BOYS!

GAH!

WHOOPS! ABOUT OUTTA RUNWAY.

COME BACK HERE--

--YOU RUNT?

ZIP!
BUH-BYE!

DEAR MR COYOTE,

    WE ARE SORRY TO INFORM YOU THAT YOUR GREAT UNCLE CERVANTES HAS PASSED AWAY. YOU ARE INVITED TO THE LAW OFFICE OF SCHYSTER, SCHYSTER, DOOLEY, CHEATUM, & HOWE FOR A READING OF THE WILL.

    SINCERELY,

MR COYOTE! WELCOME! I'M WEEZLY SCHYSTER, AND THIS IS MY BROTHER CHEEZLY SCHYSTER!
INDEED.

WE ARE SO GLAD TO SEE YOU. AND WE ARE SO SORRY THAT YOUR GREAT UNCLE HAS PASSED AWAY!
INDEED.

Uhhh...
IF YOU'RE SORRY MY GREAT UNCLE DIED, WHY ARE YOU SMILING LIKE THAT?

SO SORRY! WE JUST GET SO GIDDY WHEN IT COMES TO MATTERS OF MONEY! CAN'T WAIT TO READ THE WILL.
INDEED!

AND NOW, TO READ THE WILL: "I, CERVANTES COYOTE, BEING OF SOUND MIND & BODY BEQUEATH THE FOLLOWING IN THE EVENT OF MY DEATH.

WITH THE EXCEPTION OF MY MANSION, ALL OF MY WEALTH AND WORLDLY BELONGINGS...

...ARE TO BE DONATED TO THE FOLLOWING CHARITIES..."

WHAT?! NOTHING FOR YOUR BELOVED LAWYERS?!
INDEED.

THE READING OF GREAT UNCLE CERVANTES' WILL.
"TO MY GREAT NEPHEW AND SOLE LIVING RELATIVE, QUIXOTE COYOTE, I LEAVE MY MANSION...

...ON THE CONDITION THAT HE SPENDS THREE NIGHTS ALONE IN THE MANSION.
OH YEAH, THE MANSION'S HAUNTED."

Huh.

NEATO!

THIS IS GONNA BE FUN, THREE NIGHTS IN GREAT UNCLE CERVANTES' 'HAUNTED' MANSION.

I DON'T REALLY CARE ABOUT OWNING THE MANSION OR WHATEVER. I JUST THINK THIS WILL BE INTERESTING.

PLUS, IT'S NOT LIKE THE MANSION IS ACTUALLY HAUNTED.

GHOSTS SMOSTS.

NIGHT 1 IN THE HAUNTED HOUSE.
ALRIGHT, I'VE GOT ALL THE CANDLES LIT, & NOW I'VE GOT THE FIREPLACE GOING.

THAT SHOULD GIVE ME PLENTY OF LIGHT.

YEAH, THIS IS A NEAT OLD HOUSE.

♪ ♪ ♪

YEE-IPE!
RAH!
CHOP.!

UNH! UNH!

Sooo... YOU'RE STUCK, RIGHT?
UH...KINDA LOOKS LIKE IT.

JUST CHECKIN'.
POW

HEY THERE, MR SKELETON MAN. WHAT'S THE DEAL?

WHY'D YOU TRY TO CHOP ME UP WITH AN AXE?

NUTHIN' PERSONAL, MAN. THIS IS A HAUNTED HOUSE, IT'S THE JOB OF ALLA US UNDEAD TO TRY'N OFF YOU.

THE HAUNTED HOUSE, AROUND 10 PM.

WE MUST BE VERY QUIET BROTHER CHEEZLY. WE DON'T WANT THAT FOOL, QUIXOTE COYOTE, TO KNOW WE'RE HERE.
INDEED.

SINCE CERVANTES COYOTE DIDN'T LEAVE ANYTHING TO US, HIS BELOVED LAWYERS, IN HIS WILL, THEN WE HAVE NO CHOICE BUT TO DRESS UP AS GHOSTS, SCARE OFF QUIXOTE, AND CLAIM THIS MANSION FOR OURSELVES!
INDEED!
NOW LET'S GO SCARE THAT COYOTE!
INDEED.

NOW TO FIND THAT COYOTE AND SCARE HIM AWAY.
INDEED.

So, THE SHYSTER BROTHERS WANNA SCARE ME, HUH? WELL, TWO CAN PLAY AT THAT GAME.

HEY THERE, MR. SKULL FACE GUY, WANNA SCARE A COUPLE OF IDIOTS?
OOO! YOU KNOW I WANNA!

HEE!

Uhhh...

Boo?

GHOSTS!
INDEED!

THANKS FOR HELPING ME OUT, MR. SKULLFACEMAN.
SURE KID. I HAD FUN SCARIN' OFF THEM WEEZLES.

LISSEN, KID, I GOT SOME ADVICE FOR YA. GET OUTA THIS MANSION NOW BEFORE IT'S TOO LATE.

AROUND MIDNIGHT THIS WHOLE PLACE IS GONNA GO COMPLETELY INSANE. IT WON'T BE SAFE, SO YOU BETTER GET OUT.

NAH. I'M HAVING FUN.
YOU ARE A CRAZY COYOTE.

ACCORDING TO MR. SKULLFACEMAN, THIS PLACE IS SUPPOSED TO GET CRAZY AROUND MIDNIGHT.

WELP, IT'S AROUND MIDNIGHT...

...AND I DON'T SEE NUTHIN'.

MEOW.

So, uh, Hey There Guys. How's it Goin'?

WE ARE HUNGRY.

HUNGRY, Huh? WELL, HECK, LET'S JUST ORDER US A PIZZA, RIGHT?

OH, WE THINK WE'LL JUST EAT IN.

KICK!

MWROWR

MEOW?
MEOW?

Huh.
...
WELP, THAT WAS WEIRD.

WHEW! GOTTA ADMIT, IT'S BEEN A CRAZY NIGHT!

TALKING SKELETONS WITH AXES.

CREEPY GHOST CAT THINGIES.

OH WELL... IT CAN'T POSSIBLY GET ANY WORSE!

HAUNTED HOUSE — NIGHT ONE... STILL
RunRunRun!

YIPE!
SNAP!

OKAY, SO THE HAUNTED MANSION IS BECOMING LESS FUN.

OH! HEY!

TOLDJA YA SHOULDA LEFT THE MANSION.
NOW'S NOT THE TIME MR. SKULLFACE MAN!

GRRR!
HEY BOY! YOU WANNA BONE? FETCH BOY, FETCH BOY!
HEY! THAT'S MY LEG!

GO FETCH!

...
...
...

GRRR!
YOU REALLY THOUGHT THAT WOULD WORK?
IT ALWAYS WORKS IN THE CARTOONS!

GRRR!
SORRY MR. SKULLFACE MAN!
WAIT! WHAT ARE YOU DOING?

I'M A CREEPY GHOST SKULL THING, NOT A BASEBALL!

PLONK!

ZIP!

HA! MY BACKPACK!

WHERE IS IT?
WHERE IS IT?
WHERE IS IT?

HA! MY CANTEEN!

ROWR!

THIRSTY? HAVE SOME WATER?

SPLASH!

HiSSSS!!

AWOO!

AND SO, DAWN BREAKS, & THE NIGHT ENDS.

WELL, THE NIGHT IS OVER. AM I SAFE, MR. SKULL FACE MAN?
YEAH, YER GOOD, KID.

BUT I'D GET OUTTA HERE BEFORE TOMORROW NIGHT.

MEH.
WHAT'D BE THE FUN IN THAT?

AS OUR HERO, QUIXOTE COYOTE, SLEEPS PEACEFULLY INSIDE THE HAUNTED HOUSE...
Z.
... LET'S CHECK IN WITH SOME OTHER RESIDENTS OF CROWNVILLE.
WOLF

LA-DEE-DA!
WANDA WOLF, TODAY IS GOING TO BE A GOOD DAY!

INSIDE THE WOLF HOUSEHOLD...
YEAH! THAT STUPID QUIXOTE COYOTE IS STAYIN' AT THE HAUNTED MANSION FOR THREE NIGHTS!
?

SO, WE'RE GONNA SNEEK INTO THE MANSION AN' SCARE THE PANTS OFFA THAT SHRIMP!

MEET UP WITH ME AN' THE RESTA THE BOYS AT THE MANSION AT NIGHTFALL. COOL. BYE!

WALDO WOLF! WHAT NONSENSE ARE YOU UP TO?
EEYIPE!

THE WOLF HOUSEHOLD.
DANGIT, LITTLE SIS WANDA! DON'T YOU GO MESSIN' IN MY BUSINESS!
WHEN YOUR BUSINESS IS TROUBLE, I SHOULD INTERFERE, WALDO!
AND WHY DO YOU WANT TO GO MESSING WITH QUIXOTE COYOTE, ANYWAY?
GRRR!

THAT LITTLE RUNT GAVE ME THIS BLACK EYE!
HMPH! KNOWING YOU, YOU PROBABLY DESERVED IT.

AND SO WE BID FAREWELL TO THE WOLF HOUSEHOLD.
NOW DON'T GO CAUSING TROUBLE FOR QUIXOTE COYOTE, WALDO!
YER NOT THE BOSS'A ME, WANDA!

IN THE MEANTIME, OUR HERO, QUIXOTE COYOTE, IS STILL ASLEEP ON THE FLOOR OF THE (CURRENTLY DORMANT) HAUNTED HOUSE.
SNORE!

SO, LET'S CHECK IN WITH THE MOST HAPPY-GO-LUCKY RESIDENT OF CROWNVILLE...
HYUCK-HYUCK! I GOTS AN AUTOGRAPHED BASEBALL, AN ALL IT TOOK WAS ALL MY MONEY!
SUCKER!

...AND THE LEAST.
WORLD AIN'T NUTHIN' BUT A BUNCHA JERKS AN' LOSERS.

Doop-da-Doop! What a lovely day!

Grumble! Gripe! What a crummy day!

Hey there, Sancho! Great day, right, buddy?
What are you so happy about, Panda? What's so great about today?

CHECK IT OUT, SANCHO OLE BUDDY OLE PAL! I GOTS ME A BASEBALL AUTOGRAPHED BY TOMMY 'SLUGGER' HOLMES!

PFT!
LEMME TAKE A LOOK AT THIS 'FANCY BASEBALL' OF YOURS, PANDA.

PANDA, YOU CHOWDERHEAD! THIS AUTOGRAPH IS A FAKE! THE NAME'S NOT EVEN SPELLED RIGHT!

AW SHUCKS, SANCHO, THAT DON'T MEAN NUTHIN'! I SPELL MY NAME WRONG ALL THE TIME!
YOU HURT MY HEAD SO MUCH.

HEY SANCHO, HAVE YA SEEN QUIXOTE COYOTE?
PFT.
THAT IDIOT'S SPENDING THREE NIGHTS IN A HAUNTED HOUSE FOR SOME STUPID REASON.

WHY YOU BEIN' MEAN TO QUIXOTE FOR? WE'RE ALL PALS!
THAT JERK AIN'T NO FRIEND OF MINE!

WHADAYA MEAN? WHY AIN'T YOU AN' QUIXOTE PALS?
I'M A ROADRUNNER AND HE'S A COYOTE! WE'RE NATURAL ENEMIES!

I THINK YOU BEEN WATCHIN' TOO MANY CARTOONS.
THPBBT!

AS THE SUN SETS, WE RETURN TO THE HAUNTED MANSION...

...AND OUR HERO, QUIXOTE COYOTE.
WELP, IT'S NIGHT TWO ARE YOU GOING TO GO EASY ON ME TONIGHT, HAUNTED HOUSE?

SURE. WHY NOT?
REALLY?

NO. NOT REALLY.

NIGHT TWO IN THE HAUNTED MANSION...
ALRIGHT. FIREPLACE IS LIT.

AND THAT'S THE LAST OF THE CANDLES.

NOTHING LEFT TO DO BUT HANG OUT...
...AND WAIT FOR SOMETHING HORRIBLE TO HAPPEN.

BOOGA-BOOGA!
Oh MAN! Oh MAN! GOTTA THINK FAST!

IEEEEEEEE
?

EEEEE!!
SANCHO?

CLONK!

OW! S'ANCHO? WHAT ARE YOU--
GHOSTS! THERE'S GHOSTS EVERYWHERE!!
OF COURSE. IT'S A HAUNTED HOUSE.
IF THIS HOUSE IS FULL OF GHOSTS, THEN WHAT ARE YOU DOING HERE?!
I DUNNO. IT'S KINDA FUN, I GUESS.
I DON'T UNDERSTAND YOU AT ALL.

So, Sancho, what are you doing in this haunted house, anyway?

Pft. I heard about you stayin' in this stupid house, and I came to make fun of you. How was I supposed to know this place was ACTUALLY HAUNTED.

Sancho, why are you always so mean to me?
You're a coyote, I'm a roadrunner! We're natural enemies!

If we aren't friends, then where's that 5 bucks you owe me?
5 bucks? What're ya talkin' about? What's a little money between friends, old buddy old pal!

HELP!!!
?

WHY ARE WE RUNNING TOWARDS THE SCREAMING?

HEY THERE, FELLAS! GOOD TO SEE YA, QUIXOTE! I WANTED TO SHOW YA THE AUTOGRAPHED BASEBALL I GOT!
PANDA?!

HEY QUIXOTE! I WANTED TO SHOW YA MY AUTOGRAPHED BASEBALL, BUT THIS FELLA GRABBED ME!

YIIIKKEES!!

COME ON SANCHO! WE GOTTA CATCH PANDA!
I'M COMIN'! I'M COMIN'!

OOF!
THUD!

HEY QUIXOTE! CHECK OUT MY OH-FISH-EE-AL AUTO-GRAPHED BASEBALL!
RUN. RUN. RUN.
NO TIME RIGHT NOW, PANDA!

WE GOTTA RUN!

SO, WHAT'RE WE RUNNIN' FOR, FELLAS?

BECAUSE WE'RE BEIN' CHASED BY A GHOST, YOU CHOWDER-HEAD!
Oh yeah!

WOO-HOO-HOO!
I'M KICKIN' INTO OVERDRIVE!

BAM
ZIP
GAH!

FWOO
FSOO

SANCHO, YOU SAVED US!
I DID WHAT NOW?

CHECK OUT MY GEN-YOU-WINE AUTOGRAPHED BASEBALL, QUIXOTE!
LET ME SEE THAT, PANDA...

IS TOMMY 'SLUGGER' HOLMES HERE?
?

HELLO THERE. I'M TOMMY 'SLUGGER' HOLMES.

IS THIS YOUR AUTOGRAPH?
NOPE, IT'S A FAKE.
GOSHDARNIT.
TOLDJA.

SORRY YOUR AUTOGRAPHED BASEBALL WAS A FAKE, PANDA.
UH...
BRAINS.
OR WHATEVER.
POW!
AW, I DUNNO. IT HAS ITS USES.
HEY GUYS! THAT HURT!

TO RECAP: IN ORDER TO INHERIT HIS GREAT-UNCLE'S MANSION (WHICH IS HAUNTED) QUIXOTE COYOTE MUST SPEND 3 NIGHTS INSIDE THE MANSION. THIS IS NIGHT 2. HIS TWO FRIENDS, SANCHO AND PANDA HAVE STUMBLED IN FOR REASONS OF THEIR OWN...
IT'S BEEN REALLY FUN HAVING YOU GUYS HERE, BUT ACCORDING TO THE WILL, I'M SUPPOSED TO BE HERE ALONE. YOU SHOULD PROBABLY LEAVE.

PFT!
DON'T GOTTA TELL ME TWICE!

ZIP--CRASH

YOU REALLY NEED TO WATCH WHERE YOU'RE GOING.
AWWWW SHADDUP!

OUTSIDE THE HAUNTED MANSION...
ALRIGHT, BOYS! WE'RE GONNA SNEAK INTO THE MANSION AN' SCARE THE PANTS OFFA QUIXOTE COYOTE!
SURE THING, WALDO!

EEEEEEEEE
WHAT TH--
?

EEEE EEE!

Uhhh-- DID ANYONE GET THE NUMBER OF THAT TRUCK?

HEY THERE FELLAS! DID YOU SEE MY PAL SANCHO RUN THROUGH HERE?
WHO THE HECK 'R YOU?

THAT'S PANDA JACKRABBIT. HIS FAMILY HAS A FARM NEAR MY FAMILY. HE'S PALS WITH QUIXOTE COYOTE.
THAT'S ME!

SO, YOU'RE FRIENDS WITH THAT STUPID QUIXOTE AND THAT RUNT THAT RUN US OVER?
YEPPIR.

DO ME A FAVOR N' HOLD STILL, WOULD'JA?
OKIE-DOKIE!

POW!

Whuh?
CREEK

POW! SPROING

WELP, SEE YA AROUND, GUYS!
OW! WHAT JUST HAPPENED ?!?

THE HAUNTED MANSION - NIGHT TWO - STILL.
HUH. LOOKS LIKE THE FIREPLACE WENT OUT.

RUMBLE!
WHUH?

THUMP
FLOP!

HEY KID. YOU SEEN MY LEGS?
I-uh-I HONESTLY CAN SAY I HAVE NOT.

HEY LOOK! IT'S MY LEGS!

HEY BUDDY. YA MIND HELPIN' ME PUT MY LEGS BACK ON?
UHHH... SURE.

AW MAN! YOUR LEGS ARE SQUIRMING!
CAREFUL NOW!

UHHHHH... I DON'T THINK THIS IS RIGHT.
SORRY.

YIPE! MORE BODIES!

UH...HEY GUYS. YOU'RE NOT GONNA EAT MY FLESH, ARE YOU?

EAT YER FLESH? DON'T BE RIDICULOUS!

IT'S BOWLING NIGHT.

BOWLING NIGHT AT THE HAUNTED MANSION.

BOOM!

GRAH! I GOT A 7-10 SPLIT!
Whadaripoff.

HERE'S YOUR BOWLING BALL, QUIXOTE COYOTE.
Uh--OKAY.

OH WOW! MR. SKULLFACE MAN!

HEY KID! YOU'RE STILL ALIVE! THAT'S SO COOL!

SOOOO... DO YOU KNOW THAT YOU'RE MY BOWLING BALL?
I'M WHAT NOW?

WHADDAYA MEAN I'M YER BOWLIN' BALL?

SORRY, MR SKULLFACE MAN. I'M BOWLING WITH THESE ZOMBIE-GHOST-THINGS, AND THEY SAID YOU'RE MY BALL.

C'MON, KID! WE'RE PALS! YOU CAN'T TOSS ME DOWN THE LANE!

I DON'T HAVE A CHOICE. I'M STILL AFRAID THESE GUYS ARE GONNA EAT ME IF I DON'T GO ALONG.

C'MON QUIXOTE! DON'T BOWL ME!
SORRY MR. SKULLFACE MAN.
AAAAHH!

OW! OO! OWCH! OWIE!
POW!
WOO! I GOTTA STRIKE!

AND SO, FINALLY, A NEW DAY DAWNS...

WELP, IT'S MORNING. TIME TA GO BACK TA GHOST WORLD.

ARE YOU GOING TOO, MR SKULLFACE MAN?
YEAH, 'FRAID SO, KID.

GOOD LUCK TOMORROW NIGHT, KID.
YER GONNA NEED IT!

IT'S DAYBREAK IN THE HAUNTED MANSION. WITH THE GHOSTS GONE, QUIXOTE COYOTE SLEEPS 'PEACEFULLY'.
SNORE!
MEANWHILE, ACROSS TOWN, WALDO WOLF AND HIS PACK ARE LICKING THEIR WOUNDS.
O.KAY BOYS, WE SET OUT LAST NIGHT TO SCARE QUIXOTE COYOTE, BUT SOMEHOW HIS FRIENDS BEAT US UP.

SO, TONIGHT, WE'RE GONNA TAKE OUT THAT STOOPID COYOTE ONCE AND FOR ALL.
?!?...
TONIGHT, BOYS...
I KNEW MY NO-GOOD BROTHER WAS UP TO NO-GOOD.

SANCHO! PANDA!
WANDA WOLF?

MY NO-GOOD BROTHER IS GONNA GO TO THE HAUNTED MANSION AND PUMMEL QUIXOTE COYOTE! I NEED YOU GUYS TO HELP ME STOP HIM!

OHHH NO! NO NO NO NO! I AM NOT GOING BACK TO THAT CREEPY MANSION! I AM OUT!

WE'D BE HAPPY TA HELP, WANDA!
HELP! I'M BEIN' BIRDNAPPED!
THANKS GUYS.

MEANWHILE, ACROSS TOWN...
THE LAW OFFICE OF SHYSTER & SHYSTER, DOOLEY, CHEATUM & HOWE

WELL BROTHER, TONIGHT IS THE LAST NIGHT. IF QUIXOTE COYOTE MAKES IT THROUGH THE NIGHT, HE INHERITS THE MANSION, AND WE GET NOTHING.
INDEED.

SO, IT WOULD BE A SHAME IF WE HIRED SOMEONE TO DRAG QUIXOTE COYOTE OUT OF THE MANSION.
INDEED.

SO, I JUST GOTTA RUN OFF SOME COYOTE? SOUNDS LIKE AN EASY JOB FOR FRANKO FOX.
INDEED.

AND SO, QUIXOTE COYOTE'S THIRD NIGHT IN THE HAUNTED MANSION BEGINS.

YAAWWN!

Y'KNOW, THE LAST TWO NIGHTS IN THE HAUNTED MANSION HAVEN'T BEEN SO BAD. MAYBE TONIGHT WILL BE A...

...CAKE WALK?

Uhhhh...
IS THAT YOU UP THERE, MR SKULL-FACE MAN?

HEY KID! WHADAYA THINK OF MY NEW BODY?

WELL...THAT DEPENDS.
ON WHAT?

IT DEPENDS ON WHAT YOU PLAN ON DOING WITH THAT BIG HONKIN' AXE.

LOOK ON THE BRIGHT SIDE, QUIXOTE.

AFTER I CHOP YOU UP, YOU'LL BECOME A GHOST!

SO WE CAN HANG OUT AND BE PALS FOREVER!

WON'T THAT BE COOL, QUIXOTE?
...
QUIXOTE?

IT'S NUTHIN' PERSONAL, QUIXOTE!

I JUST GOTTA CHOP YOU UP!

SEEMS PRETTY PERSONAL TO ME!!!

YIKES!
CRASH!

UH, KID?

WHATCHA DOIN'?

BOOT

DE JA VUUUUuuu!

SOOOO... YOU'RE NOT MAD AT ME FOR TRYIN' TO CHOP YOU UP WITH A GIANT AXE, RIGHT?
NOTHIN' PERSONAL, RIGHT QUIXOTE?

WE'RE COOL, RIGHT BUDDY?

GUESS NOT!
PUNT!

EEEEEEE
?

EEEEEEE
NOW THAT I THINK ABOUT IT...

EEEEEEE
...SHOULD I REALLY BE RUNNING TOWARD THE SCREAMING?

EE EEE!
SANCHO & PANDA? What're they doing back here?
BOO!
BWAHAHA!

EEEEEEEEEE!!
BOO-HA-HA!
GONNA GETCHA!
BOO-EEEYIPEE!

HEY THERE BUDDY! WE WUZ JUST MESSIN' AROUND. WE WEREN'T GONNA HURT NOBODY! SO WHY DON'T YOU PUT THAT CANDLE--
--AWAYIIEEE!!!

The Haunted House — Night 3. Quixote Coyote, Sancho, & Panda Reunited.

WHAT ARE YOU GUYS DOING HERE?!?

EEEEEK!!!

WHAT WAS THAT?
PROBABLY WANDA WOLF GETTIN' CHASED BY GHOSTS OR SOMETHIN'!

YOU DRAGGED WANDA INTO THIS PLACE?!?
NO, SHE DRAGGED ME HERE!!!

I CAN'T BELIEVE YOU GUYS BROUGHT WANDA TO THIS HAUNTED HOUSE.

HEY! I DIDN'T WANNA COME HERE! PANDA DRAGGED ME HERE!

SORRY.
THERE SHE IS!

HELP!!!!
Yummy!

HEY STUPID GHOST! WHY WASTE YOUR TIME WITH A TINY MORSEL LIKE HER, WHEN YOU CAN CHOW DOWN ON THREE MEATY GUYS LIKE US?!?
QUIXOTE?

Hmmm---

NO OFFENCE, MA'AM, BUT HE DOES HAVE A POINT.

WHAT IS WRONG WITH YOU?!?

HEY SANCHO, WHY YOU RUNNIN' SO SLOW?
WHAT'RE YOU TALKIN' ABOUT?

ACTUALLY, PANDA'S GOT A POINT. YOU'RE A SUPER-FAST RUNNER.
NOW'S NOT THE TIME, GUYS!

...

YOU'RE JUST AFRAID YOU'LL GET LOST AND THEN BE ALONE IN THE HAUNTED HOUSE.
WILL YOU TWO SHUT UP!

YES! THERE'S MY LUNCH!

EAT UP, PAL!

CHOMP-CHOMP-MUNCH-MUNCH!

MM- THAT WAS TASTY!

THANKS AGAIN FOR THE MEAL.
HOW DID YOU KNOW THAT WOULD WORK?
POOF!
HE WAS HUNGRY, SO I FED HIM.

OKAY. GREAT. BUT HOW DID YOU KNOW THAT WOULD WORK?!?
EH. LUCKY GUESS.
STICK A FORK IN ME, I'M DONE.

QUIXOTE!
WANDA!

♥

SLAP!

WHY ARE YOU STAYING IN SUCH A DANGEROUS PLACE?!?
WHUH?

OKAY, SERIOUSLY, YOU GUYS NEED TO LEAVE THIS PLACE!
THAT'S WHAT I WANTED TO DO ALL ALONG!

?
I'M NOT LEAVING HERE WITHOUT YOU!

TOMP!

WE ARE ALL GOING TO LEAVE THIS MANSION IN A CALM AND ORDERLY FASHION, AND NO ONE WILL GET HURT. UNDERSTAND?
GRR!
!!!
EEK!

I'M GETTING PAID REALLY GOOD MONEY TO GET YOU OUT OF THIS HOUSE, SO THAT'S WHAT WE'RE GOING TO DO.
I'M COOL WITH THAT!
I SWEAR, IF YOU HARM SO MUCH AS A HAIR ON HER HEAD, I'M GONNA--

LET--ME--
--GO!

I'LL TAKE OUT THE BIG GUY FIRST.
SANCHO, LOOK OUT FOR WANDA WHILE I DEAL WITH MR FOX!
SURE!

POW!

AUGH! WHAT'S YOUR HEAD MADE OUT OF? CONCRETE?!?
HEY GUYS! WHUT'S GOIN' ON? I SPACED OUT.

PANDA, GO OVER THERE WITH SANCHO & WANDA. I'M GONNA TEACH THIS MERCENARY A LESSON!
OKEE-DOKEE QUIXOTE! HAVE FUN!

KICK!
LUCKY SHOT.

BOOM!

CRASH!

NOW I'M MAD!

RAA!

HOW ARE YOU STILL STANDING?

POWPOWPOWPOW!!

BOOM
'CAUSE WHEN YOU'RE A LITTLE GUY, YOU GOTTA KNOW HOW TO TAKE A BEATING!

WHO HIRED YOU?

A PROFESSIONAL NEVER RATS OUT HIS EMPLOYERS!

POW!
WHOEVER THEY ARE--

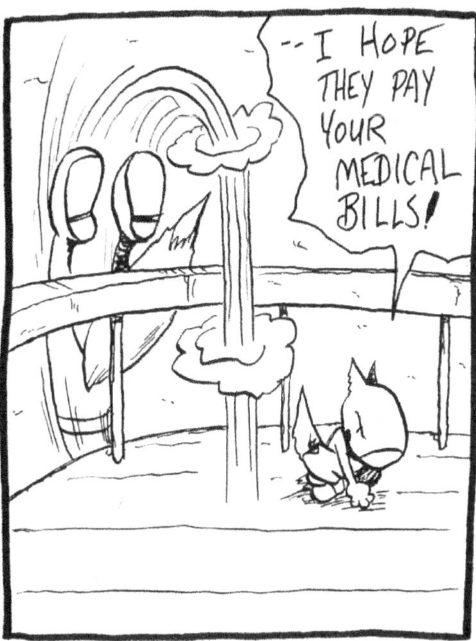

--I HOPE THEY PAY YOUR MEDICAL BILLS!

WHEW! THAT FOX COULD FIGHT!
WHAT'S GOING ON ?!?
DUDE. IT'S A HAUNTED HOUSE.
HELP MEEE!!!
PASS.

OUTSIDE THE HAUNTED MANSION...
ALRIGHT BOYS! TIME TO GET OUR REVENGE ON QUIXOTE COYOTE!

GET ME OUT OF HERE!
CRASH

IT'S HAUNTED! HAUNTED I TELL YA!

UH...I DUNNO 'BOUT THIS, WALDO.
AW SHADDUP AND GET INSIDE, YA BIG CHICKEN!

YOU OKAY, QUIXOTE?
THAT FOX REALLY PUT UP A FIGHT.
JUST NEED A SECOND TO CATCH MY BREATH.

THAT TAKES CARE OF THOSE TWO GOOFBALLS, WALDO. BUT WHAT ABOUT YOUR SISTER?
MFF!
MFF!
OH, YOU LET ME WORRY ABOUT "LIL' SIS."

GET 'IM BOYS!

GET READY FOR A POUNDIN' RUNT!

BIG BROTHER, WHY ARE YOU SUCH A NO-GOOD JERK?

WHAT CAN I SAY? IT'S FUN BEATING UP PEOPLE SMALLER THAN ME!
MF!

GRAB 'IM!
HYUCK!

GOTCHA!
LET-ME--

CLONK!
--GO!

HA!
POP!

YOWL!
KICK!

OW
OW!
OW!

HI THERE.

BOOM

IF YOU WANT SOMETHIN' DONE RIGHT, YOU GOTTA DO IT YERSELF!
HUFF! HUFF!

HA!
SOCK

WHUD!

ARE YOU ENJOYING THIS AS MUCH AS I AM, RUNT?

THUNK!

DAGNABBIT!
URG!

OOF!

OH FER THE
LUV OF--

THERE'S THREE
OF US, AND
ONLY ONE OF--

--HIM?

YUMMY!

WHAT HAPPENED? WHERE ARE WE?

WE GOT EATEN BY A GIANT GHOST, AND NOW WE'RE FLOATING IN HIS GHOST STOMACH.

GHOSTS?!?

DUDE. SERIOUSLY. HAUNTED HOUSE.

EXCUSE ME, BOYS. I'M GONNA TRY SOMETHING.

WHAT'RE YOU UP TO, RUNT?
GRR!

POW!

ROW!
WHIIIIIR!!

HUH. IT'S THE GIANT GHOST'S GIANT GHOST GIANT BRAIN.

BACK OFF, MAN! DON'T MAKE ME HURT YOU!

HEY! YOU'RE THE ONE WHO ATE ME, PAL!
POW

YES SIR! SORRY SIR! ANYTHING YOU SAY, SIR!
YER DARN TOOTIN'!

FIRST WE GET ATE BY THAT BIG GHOST...
((oo))
THEN QUIXOTE COYOTE WALLOPS US AND THROWS US OUTA THE BIG GHOST!
SO, WHADDA WE DO NOW, BOSS?
BOOHAHAHA!
I'LL TELL YA WHAT TA DO: RUN!

BOOHAHAHA!
HEY WALDO!
I KINDA GET WHY YOU DO THIS.
THIS IS FUN!

WAHAHAHA!
LATER, BOYS.

TOSS!

KRISH!

POP!
UGH! I GOT SUCH A HEADACHE.
WELL YEAH, I PUNCHED YOU IN THE BRAIN AND CONTROLLED YOU LIKE A PUPPET.
POOF!
I'M GOIN' BACK TO GHOSTWORLD WHERE IT'S SAFE.
GOOD PLAN.

HURRY AN' GET ME OUTA THIS!
CALM DOWN, SANCHO.
ALRIGHT, NOW YOU GUYS NEED TO GET OUT OF HERE.
DON'T GOTTA TELL ME TWICE! C'MON, PANDA!
SEE YA QUIXOTE!
YOU BE CAREFUL. DON'T DO ANYTHING STUPID, STUPID.
YOU WORRY TOO MUCH, WANDA.
AND YOU DON'T WORRY ENOUGH. I BALANCE US OUT.

WELP, EVERYONE'S GONE. JUST ME ALONE IN THE HAUNTED HOUSE.

ALRIGHT, HOUSE! IT'S THE LAST NIGHT. IT'S ALMOST DAWN. WHAT'CHA GOT FOR ME?!?

OOOOOOOOO!

HELLO, QUIXOTE.
GREAT UNCLE CERVANTES!

SO, UNCLE CERVANTES... HOW YA BEEN?

WELL... I'M DEAD.

...
...

BUT OTHER THAN THAT, I'M GOOD.
...
THAT'S COOL.

ACTUALLY, KID, GHOSTWORLD IS PRETTY OKAY.

LOTS OF OTHER GHOSTS TO HANG OUT WITH, LOTS OF STUFF TO DO. I'M ON A BOWLING TEAM. WE'RE PRETTY OKAY.

NO TACOS, THOUGH.

I DO MISS TACOS.

SOOO...
...HOW ARE MY MOM & DAD?

OH. YOUR PARENTS AREN'T IN GHOSTWORLD.

OH WAIT! I DIDN'T MEAN IT LIKE THAT, KIDDO!

YOUR PARENTS LEFT GHOSTWORLD, AND THEY'RE OFF EXPLORING OTHER DIMENSIONS. YOU KNOW HOW THEY ARE, ALWAYS LOOKING FOR ANOTHER ADVENTURE.
YEAH.

WE COYOTES HAVE ALWAYS BEEN AN ADVENTUROUS BUNCH.

THAT'S WHY I SET UP THIS WHOLE INHERITENCE SCENARIO.

I NEEDED TO KNOW WHAT KIND OF COYOTE YOU ARE.

I'M VERY PROUD OF YOU, QUIXOTE. YOU'VE HANDLED YOURSELF ADMIRABLY THESE LAST 3 NIGHTS IN THE HAUNTED HOUSE.
AW...THANKS, GREAT UNCLE CERVANTES.

SOO... UNCLE CERVANTES... HOW DID YOU... Y'KNOW... PASS?

A LIFETIME OF GRAND ADVENTURES ACROSS THE GLOBE.

DECADES SPENT LIVING IN A HAUNTED MANSION.

AND... I ACCIDENTALLY CHOKED ON A HAM SANDWHICH.

SO, I GUESS THIS PLACE IS MINE NOW, RIGHT UNCLE CERVANTES?

SORRY, QUIXOTE. THIS PLACE IS TOO DANGEROUS. I MEAN, KIDS COULD GET IN HERE.
YEAH, THAT WOULD BE BAD.

SO, I'M GONNA PULL THIS PLACE INTO GHOSTWORLD WITH ME AND SEAL THE PATH BETWEEN WORLDS.

EH. I HONESTLY DON'T THINK I COULD AFFORD THE REAL ESTATE TAXES ON THIS PLACE ANYWAY.

SO... IS THIS GOODBYE, UNCLE CERVANTES?

I'M AFRAID SO, QUIXOTE. IT'S ALMOST DAWN, AND ALL US GHOSTS GOTTA GO AWAY IN THE DAWN.

IT WAS GOOD SEEING YOU AGAIN, GREAT UNCLE.

NEVER STOP HAVING ADVENTURES, KID.

Hummm

WOOO!

SHOOP!
WELP, THERE GOES MY INHERITENCE.

POP!
AND NOW I'M OFF TO BED FOR 3 DAYS.

Check out more of Quixote Coyote's Adventures at

www.torcpress.com

If you like our comics, help support us at

www.patreon.com/josephmorris_torcpress

The Official Podcast of TORC Press is

http://www.twobrosthreethings.podbean.com/

The 2 Bros 3 Things Podcast is Recorded at 3HD Studios.
Check them out for all of your Recording Needs:

https://3hdrecording.com/